This book belongs to

....

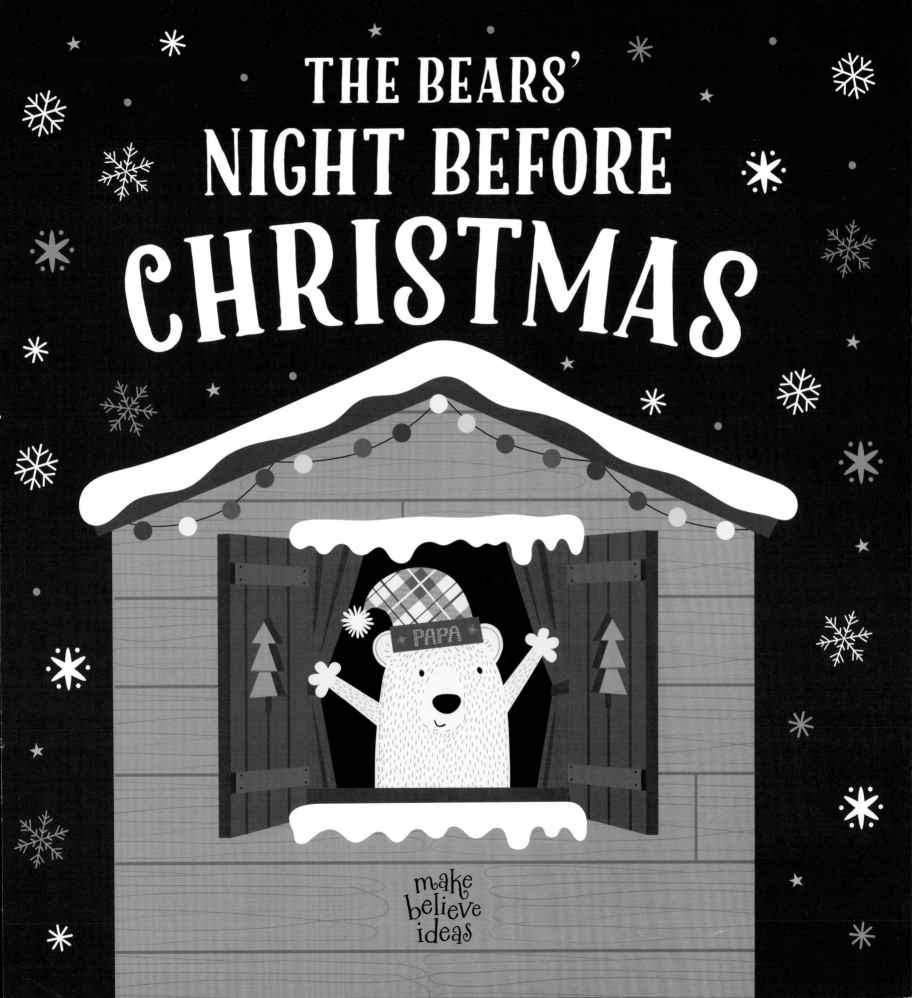

'Twas the **night** before Christmas,
at *quarter to ten*,
and my family and I
all **snoozed** in our *den*.

The stockings were hung
by the chimney with care—

for Lil' and Mama and me, Papa Bear!

Lil' Bear was nestled all snug in his bed,
while visions of honeycomb danced in his head.

And Mama in her 'kerchief, and I in my cap,
had just settled down for a long winter's nap.

When out in the woods there arose such a clatter,
I opened an eye to see what was the matter.

Outside the window I noticed a flash,

so I pawed at the shutters...

...and threw up the sash.

The moon on the top of the new-fallen snow,
gave the shimmer of sunshine to objects below.

When, what to my beady old
eyes should appear ...

...but a **miniature** *sleigh* and **eight tiny** *reindeer!*

With a little old **driver**, so *lively* and **quick**,
I knew in a **moment** it must be *St. Nick.*

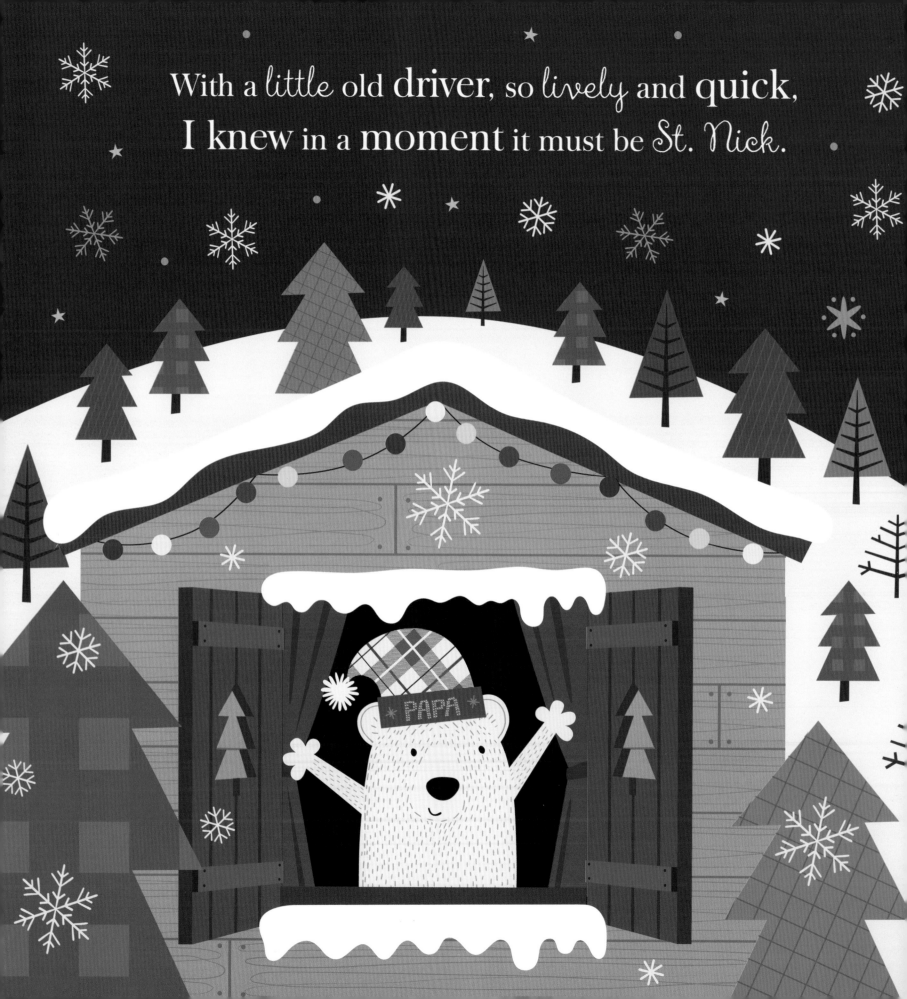

More rapid than **eagles**
his *sleigh* team all came,
and he *whistled* and *shouted*
and called them by name.

"Now, Dasher! Now, Dancer!
Now, Prancer and Vixen!

On, Comet! On, Cupid!
On, Donner and Blitzen!

To each creature's **house**, from the **big** to the *small* –
dash away! Dash away! Dash away all!"

As dry leaves that before
the wild hurricane fly,
when they meet with an obstacle,
mount to the sky;
so up to the housetops
the reindeer they flew,
with a sleigh full of toys,
and St. Nicholas too.

And then, in a *twinkling*, I heard on the roof
the **prancing** and **pawing** of each little *hoof*.

As I *drew* in my paw, and was **turning around**,
down the chimney St. Nicholas came with a bound.

He wasn't a **bear**,
but an *old man* instead,
and he *dressed head to toe*
in **bright, robin red.**

He looked like some sort of *strange* lumberjack,
with *big shiny boots* and a **load** on his **back.**

His eyes – how they *twinkled!*
His dimples – so *merry!*
His cheeks were like *roses,*
his nose like a *cherry!*

His droll little mouth
was drawn up like a *bow,*
and the beard on his chin
was as white as the *snow.*

He had a **broad face** and a *little round* **belly,**
that **shook** when he *laughed,* like a **bowlful** of *jelly!*

He was *chubby* and **plump**, a right *jolly* old elf,
and I *laughed* when I saw him, in spite of myself.

A wink of his eye and a
twist of his head,
soon gave me to know I had
nothing to dread.

He spoke not a word, but
went straight to his work,
and filled all the stockings,
then turned with a jerk.

He **sprang** to his *sleigh*, to his **team** gave a *whistle*, and **away** they all *flew*, like the **down** of a *thistle*.

But I **heard** him *exclaim,*
as he **drove** out of *sight ...*

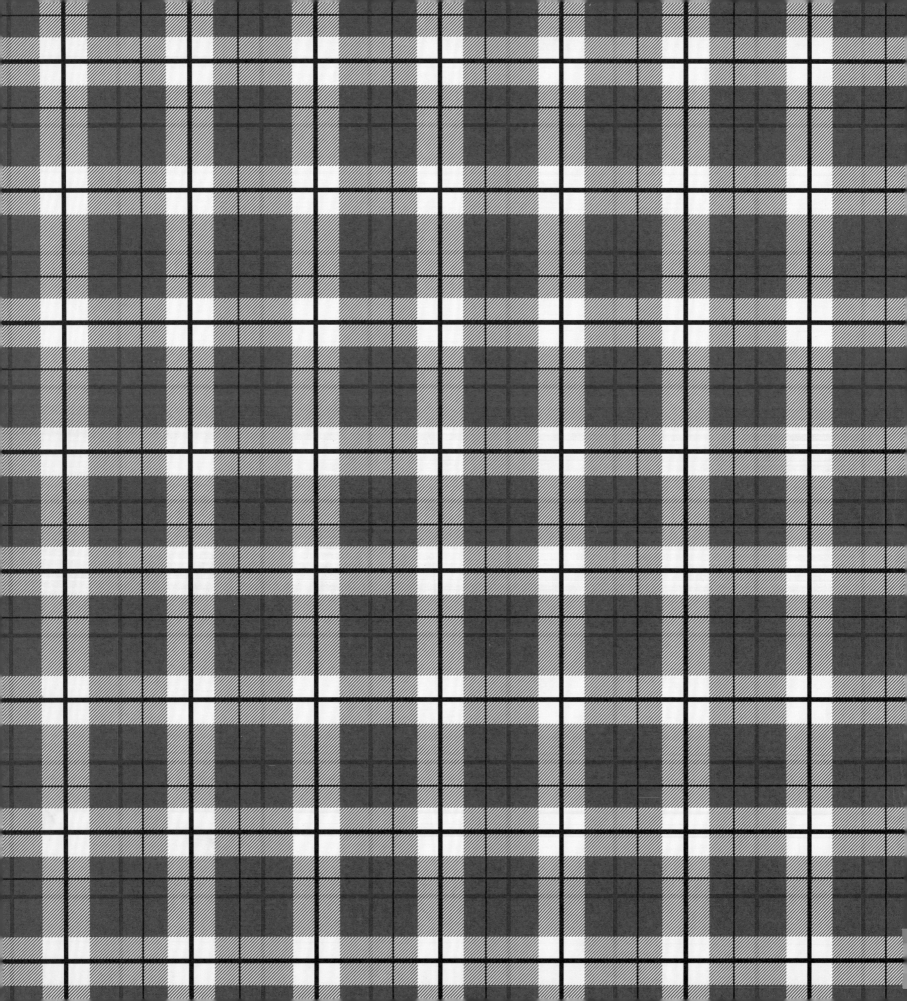